THE BROWN PAPER BAG

The Adventures of Hunter & Ramona Pug Series
Based on a True Story

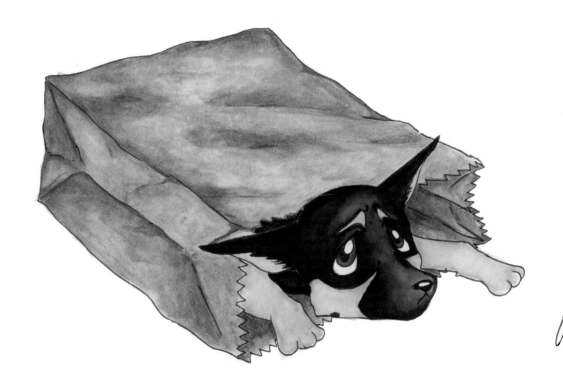

Written by Destry Ramey

Illustrated by Jesus Chavez

It is important to recognize the value of the gifts you hold in your hand.
The most amazing treasures come from the least likely places.

This book is dedicated to Feather and "All Animals in Need"

Acknowledgements

My son, Chris Ramey, who made this book possible
Jesus Chavez, for his dedication, hard work and creativity
Judy Guarnera, Susan Tuttle and Anna Unkovich for their editing expertise
My sister, Cheryl Lehman and my son, Chris for their final edits

Meet Feather and the pugs at:
www.Thepugs.com

Copyright 2015 by Destry Ramey
All rights reserved

Illustrations by Jesus Chavez
http://jchavezart.tumblr.com

ISBN: 978-1-930401-29-7

Library of Congress Control Number: 2015948531

Central Coast Press
San Luis Obispo, CA

Production Date: September 2015
Plant & Location: Printed by We SP Corp., Seoul, Korea
Batch # 54831-0

Chapter 1: Mystery Bag

The pugs position themselves in their beds on the front porch. Egress scratches and paws at her blanket, moving it back and forth until it's bunched up perfectly. Ramona sniffs the crisp night air for faded scents of the day. Kippy's legs move swiftly as she flits through the pasture of a dream.
Hunter lies in his bed with his eyes fixed on Daddy Chris.

"Hey Little Buddy," says Chris, looking up from his book. "Do you want to sit on Daddy's lap?" Hunter's tail happily drums the porch. He leaps into Chris' lap, curls up and snorts a soft, doggy purr.

Vroom. Vroom. Screech. Squeal!
Ramona's ears prick up at the sound of tires screeching
from the road below. She jumps from her bed and
sails over the steps on her short pug legs.
She crunches through leaves as she crosses
the grass and stops at the edge of her yard.

A brown paper bag flies from the window
of a dark car that zooms down the hill.
The bag spins, flips and bounces into the
street. It crashes against the curb.

When Ramona sees the bag, visions of yummy treats whirl in her head. She races to the curb, drool dripping from the sides of her mouth and sniffs the bag. The bag moves.

Rustle, crunckle, crinkle, crunch. Crinkle, crunckle, rustle, crunch!

"Yikes!" Ramona shrieks and jumps back.

Hunter hears his sister's cry and jumps off Chris' lap.

He runs lickety-split to Ramona's side with Kippy and Egress trailing close behind.

Ramona stares wide-eyed at the paper bag. Her knees are trembling.

"What's wrong, Ramona?" asks Hunter.

"The . . . the bag. The food . . . the food in the bag. It moves."

"Oh, Ramona!" Hunter says, a ghost of a smile on his lips. "Food can't move."

"This food moves!" she says.

Rustle, crunckle, crinkle, crunch. Crinkle, crunckle, rustle, crunch!

"See!" she gasps.

Hunter gently nudges the bag with his nose. The bag falls on its side.

Rustle, crunckle, crinkle, crunch. Crinkle, crunckle, rustle, crunch!

A black pointed nose emerges. Ramona steps back, her legs now like Jello.

Velvet triangular ears stand up perfectly straight alongside a tiny head.

Tan eyebrows frame dark curious eyes that warily look around.

"Aawww, it's a puppy," says Hunter.

The puppy wriggles and squirms loose from the bag; pees, poops and shakes.

7

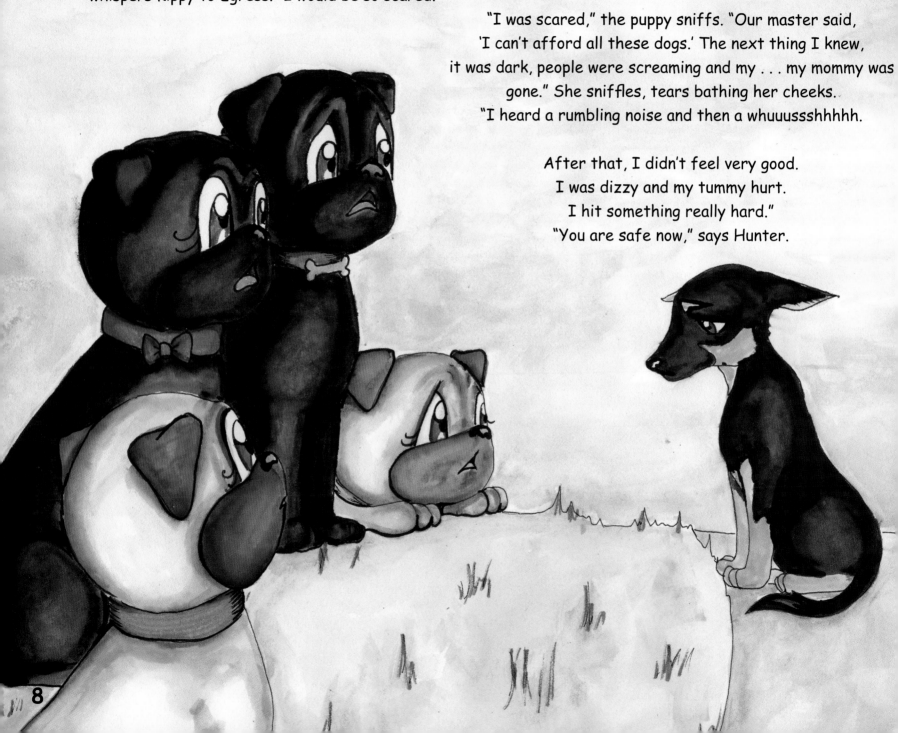

"Hi!" the puppy says in a small clear voice.
"What kind of person would throw a puppy out of a car window?"
whispers Kippy to Egress. "I would be so scared."

"I was scared," the puppy sniffs. "Our master said,
'I can't afford all these dogs.' The next thing I knew,
it was dark, people were screaming and my . . . my mommy was
gone." She sniffles, tears bathing her cheeks.
"I heard a rumbling noise and then a whuuussshhhhh.

After that, I didn't feel very good.
I was dizzy and my tummy hurt.
I hit something really hard."
"You are safe now," says Hunter.

Ramona steps forward. "Hi puppy, my name is Ramona.
This is my brother, Hunter, and these are my sisters, Kippy, and Egress."
Chris crosses the lawn to join the pugs under stars that flicker faintly in the night.
"Who do we have here?" he asks.
The pugs coax the puppy to Chris. Emotions play over her sweet face, like sunshine and clouds.

"Don't worry," says Egress. "Daddy Chris loves dogs."
Chris sits cross-legged on the curb, strokes the puppy's head and scratches behind her ears.
"You're out of harm's way now, little one," Chris says softly. He massages her small flea-infested body,
examining every inch. "You are one tough and very lucky little girl."

Chapter 2: The Foundling

Chris carries the puppy inside. He bathes her with flea shampoo,
combing any remaining fleas from her fur.
A quizzical look crosses the puppy's face as she stands rigid in the warm water.

"She looks like a little wet rat," Kippy snickers, attempting to suppress a giggle.

"Can we keep her, Daddy Chris? Please, please, pleeeeease," begs Ramona.
"I'd love to keep her, but we already meet the pet condo limit
with you four little monsters." He winks.

Chris dries the puppy and clips her tiny toenails.
"OK, munchkin, off you go," he says patting her bottom.

The puppy leaps from Chris' lap and races through the house.
She switchbacks from room to room, whizzing past
Chris and the pugs like a windup toy.
Egress blinks. "Wow! She's fast."

The puppy runs up to the pugs. "Arf, arf!" She drops down to her elbows,
lifts her rump in the air and holds her tail high. "Arf, arf, arf!"
"Look!" chuckles Ramona. "She wants to play."

Snatching a sock from beneath the couch, the puppy darts off.
She clutches the sock between her teeth and dashes toward the dining room.
Just as she reaches the doorway, the puppy skids to a stop and drops the sock.
She backs up and emits a long, low growl. "Grrrrrrrrrrrrrrr."

Stretching her neck to peek around the wall, the puppy moves
forward at a snail's pace. She steps side to side and then back again.
She bounces back and forth like a yo-yo in rhythm to her loud barks.
Frantically she paws at the image facing her in the floor-to-ceiling mirror.
The pugs howl with laughter. "She's so funny," smiles Egress.
"She thinks her reflection is another dog."

Chris lets the dogs out to the safe area of their yard.
"What should we call her?" asks Ramona.
"Let's call her Angel," says Egress. "She's so sweet."
"I like Lucky," says Hunter. "She's lucky we found her."

Kippy waves her paw. "I know-I know. Let's call her Feather!"
"Feather? What kind of name is Feather?" asks Hunter. "She's not a bird."
Ramona smiles. "Kippy remembers what our Abuela told us about feathers."
"I remember too," beams Egress. "When you see a feather, it means your angel is nearby."
The pugs glance at one another and nod in agreement.
"Feather. Perfect," says Hunter.

That night, Chris posts Feather's photo and story on Facebook.
The next morning, the pugs line up single file on the back of the couch to look out the window.
They watch Chris and Feather drive away.

Ramona's cheek glistens with freshly shed tears. "I'm really going to miss her."
"We all will," says Hunter. "Feather is a special little puppy."
"And, a pistol of fun," says Kippy, misty-eyed.

Chapter 3: The Animal Shelter

Chris gives Feather a hug and places her in the warm kennel prepared by the shelter.
"I'll see you tomorrow, little one."
Feather presses her nose between the kennel bars. Her gaze is steady as she watches Chris leave
and the door close behind him. *Why is Daddy Chris leaving me?*
Her brow wrinkles. *I thought he liked me.*

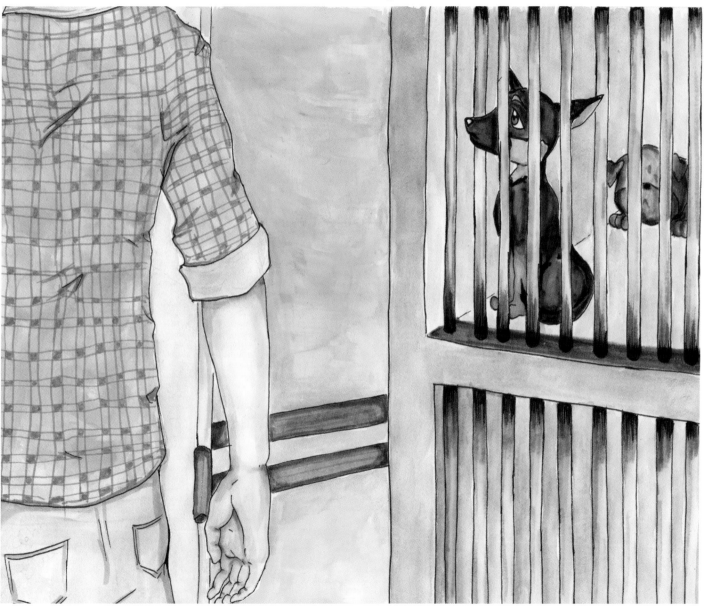

Feather hears a soft snort and turns around. A small gray pug is coiled against
the corner of the cage. Happy to see the familiar pug face, Feather forgets to be sad.

"Hi! I'm Feather. What's your name?"
"Lucy," the pug murmurs and looks up.

"Are you waiting to be adopted too?"
"Yes," Lucy sighs, "but, I don't think anybody will adopt me."
Feather raises her eyebrows. "Why not?"

"I'm thirteen years old. My hips are twisted and I can't walk very well.
Most people want a dog that can run and play with them."
"I don't care if you can't walk well.
I can walk and run for the both of us." Feather says.
"I can run really, really fast."

Feather pauses when she looks into Lucy's sad eyes.
"How long have you been here?"

"Only a couple of days," says Lucy, her eyes searching for comfort.
"I loved my Lady. I knew she was sick," sniffs Lucy.
"She kissed and cuddled me all the time."
Tears well up in Lucy's eyes and slide down her cheeks.
"Now, my—my Lady can't—take care of herself or me anymore."
"I'm so sorry, Lucy. What will you do?"

Lucy lays her head between her two front paws, "I don't know."

"Don't worry Lucy! Daddy Chris is finding me a home. I'll ask him to find you a home too."
Feather snuggles up close to Lucy and lays her head over Lucy's fragile body.
Together they fall asleep; two soft snores sound like one.

Chapter 4: A New Home

Two days later, the pugs play in the yard with Chris.
Ramona's mind shifts like a kaleidoscope that changes with every turn,
from memories to plans to feelings to worries.
"Has anyone come for Feather?" she asks.
"Not yet," answers Chris.
"It might take a few days to find a new owner for Feather."

"We must know someone who would want to adopt her," says Hunter.
He thinks about his grandmother "Abuela," Daddy Chris' mother. Hunter's eyes light up.
"What about Abuela? She would definitely love Feather."
"Definitely spoil her, too," giggles Kippy.
"Abuela is out of town so I sent her a text," says Chris.
"It is difficult for Abuela to have a dog since her job requires so much travel."

The next evening Chris greets the pugs with a twinkle in his eye.
"Who would like to see Feather before she meets her new owner?"
"You found Feather a home?" asks Hunter.
"Yes," smiles Chris. "You will be pleased."
"Who is it?" asks Kippy.

"Maybe it should be a surprise," says Chris, ruffling the fur on each pug's back.
"Or, should I tell you now?"
"Tell us now, please tell us now," begs Egress.
"Well today, your Abuela called me. She said Feather must stay in our family."
"But, how—how can she? Our condo won't allow any more dogs," says Egress.
"That's true," says Chris. "Feather will be Abuela's dog. You stay with Abuela when I travel,
and now Feather will stay with us when Abuela travels."
"Our Abuela, our very own Abuela?" The excited pugs bumper car, one into the other.

"Your Abuela will meet Feather this weekend. She'll take Feather home after her visit."
Sitting on her cinnamon bun curled tail, Kippy places her paws on her wrinkled forehead.
"I can't believe it. Our very own Abuela. Now we'll see Feather all the time. Can we tell Max?"

Max is the boy who lives next door. The pugs adore Max and they play ball with him almost every day.
"Sure," says Chris, opening the gate. The pugs burst through the gate and storm into the courtyard in search of Max.

Max relaxes under a tall pine tree in the courtyard. Light shines through the branches onto the pine needles
under his wheelchair. He gazes at the clouds and watches a squirrel skitter along a branch.
Max looks toward the sound of excited barking.

The pugs charge to him with Kippy leading the pack.
Kippy is fired up with enthusiasm, like a soap bubble about to pop.

"Guess what Max! We just learned that our Abuela is adopting Feather!
Feather will stay with us all weekend and," she huffs, "you can meet Feather
tomorrow at your birthday party." Kippy puffs again, trying to catch her breath.

"Cool," says Max and gives Kippy a high five. "I wish I could have adopted Feather.
My mom thinks a puppy would be too spirited for me. Do you want to play ball?"
Max asks pulling a ball from the bucket of balls attached to his wheelchair.

"Yes!" the pugs cheer. They race to the center of the courtyard and stand alert.
Four pairs of large eyes lock onto the ball clutched in Max's hand.
Max lifts the ball, holds it briefly in the air, then hurls it across the lawn.

The pugs scatter and trip over each other in clumsy, comical attempts to retrieve the ball.
Kippy slips, skids and falls spread-eagle facedown in the grass.
The other pugs stop. Kippy lifts her head slowly.
Feeling clever, Kippy smirks as she proudly displays the yellow ball clenched between her teeth.

Max laughs with delight. He pitches more balls, one after another until it is time for dinner.
"Thanks Max," the pugs wave as they head home.
"That was so much fun. We'll see you tomorrow with Feather."

The next morning when Feather sees Chris come through the shelter door, she bounces inside her kennel,
like a basketball dribbling down the court, and madly wags her tail.
She whimpers and scratches the kennel bars, paw over paw, with frenzied delight.
"I see you little one." Chris smiles. "Today, you're coming home with Daddy Chris.
Our Abuela is adopting you."

The kennel door barely open, Feather leaps, with an enthusiastic lunge, into Chris' arms.
"Whoa munchkin," Chris laughs, catching her and her little wet kisses.
Chris strokes Lucy's back and rubs between her ears, then closes the kennel door.

"Don't worry, Lucy," says Feather. "Daddy Chris will find you a home, too.
Remember, you're my BFF—Best Friend Forever."

Lucy's brown eyes follow Chris and Feather to the shelter door. Her forehead presses
against the kennel bars as she watches them leave and the door slowly close.

Chapter 5: Birthday Surprise

Later that afternoon, the pugs take Feather to Max's birthday party.
"C'mon, Feather," says Kippy, running through the gate. "Come meet Max."
Max wheels into the courtyard wearing a party hat and shirt that scream
'Happy Birthday.' A cluster of colorful balloons float from the back of his wheelchair.
Max holds a big gold box with a large red bow in his lap and grins from ear to ear.

"Happy Birthday Max!" the pugs shout. "We brought Feather," says Ramona. "She's part of our family now."
"Hi Feather, I'm so happy Abuela adopted you. Thank you for coming to my party."
"Wow Max! That's a huge birthday present," says Egress. "What did you get?"
"The best birthday present in the whole wide world," Max carefully lifts the lid.

The pugs peek inside the box. "That's awesome Max!
It's what you've always wanted."

Unable to see, Feather sits up on her hind legs, stretches her tiny
body and extends her neck. Dumbfounded, she stares into the box.

"Lucy! Lucy, is that really you? What are you doing here?"
"I'm Max's birthday surprise," smiles Lucy.
"Daddy Chris told Max's mom about me."

Feather dives into Max's lap and showers Lucy's face with kisses.
"I can't believe you're really here, Lucy.
Now all of us can be together, forever and ever."
Feather leaps from the wheelchair onto the lawn.

She springs across the courtyard and jumps into a pile of leaves.
She chases everything and anything that moves: falling leaves,
fluttering butterflies and dainty dandelion-seed parachutes.

Hunter watches Lucy snuggle into Max's arms and lick his cheek.
"So that's Lucy," smiles Hunter, "Feather's Lucy."

Feeling giddy and tingly all over, Feather stops
in front of Max, Lucy and the pugs.
"Today is the bestest day of my life!"

Max's guests leave when the moon comes up,
the sunset coloring the sky like the inside of a seashell.
Chris and Max relax on the porch.
Feather, Lucy and the pugs snuggle in a large dog bed nearby,
totally exhausted from their day.

Feather looks up at the full, round moon.
She is happy that she will share many more wonderful days with Lucy and the pugs.
She lays her head over Lucy's body and falls asleep; their two snores, once again, sound like one.

Chapter 6: A Day in the Park

Daddy Chris pushes Max's wheelchair through the park gardens.
Happy to be in Max's lap, Lucy enjoys the warmth of the sun on her back
as she lifts her head to catch the fragrant breeze.
The pugs stroll beside them and occasionally stop to smell a flower or investigate a bug.

Thin hazy clouds drift overhead as Kippy dilly-dallies along.
She is distracted by a bright orange butterfly, with black bordered wings that look like stained glass windows.
Kippy stumbles on a tree root. She catches herself and notices a poster stapled to the tree.

37

Kippy runs to Hunter, Ramona and Egress in a tizzy.
She darts between them, babbling and blurting out words.
"Slow down, Kippy," smiles Hunter. "What are you trying to say?"
"I saw a poster about a Chihuahua race. We could—we should—we must enter Feather!
She's fast and she's a Mixed Chihuahua."
"She does love to run," Ramona nods.

Egress raises her paw, "And—she's fast!"
"Don't forget though, Feather's only a puppy," says Hunter. "She's never run in a race."
"It's true, she's never raced," agrees Lucy, "but, she does have the heart of a racer."
The decision is made and Feather is entered in the
Chihuahuas de Mayo Race sponsored by the Humane Society.

Chihuahuas de Mayo
Sponsored by the Humane Society
Saturday, May 2 from 12-3pm
Free Admission, Chihuahua Races
Mega Adoption Event

Chapter 7: The Race

The day of the race arrives. Feather is competing against two hundred dogs.
She is the youngest, the long shot. Five year old Avatar is favored to win.
Avatar has been Grand Champion for the Humane Society for the past two years. He is strong, fast and muscular.
Max sits with Lucy and the pugs in the front row.
The pugs sit on the edge of their seats, their nails click-click-clicking against the rail as they check out the competition.
"Two hundred dogs," says Hunter. "This is a major race, especially for a puppy."

Daddy Chris briefs Feather and massages her shoulders. The bugle calls the signal for the dogs to line up at the gate.
Feather stands in her post and quickly scans the crowd to find her family. She sees them in the front row.
Big broad smiles come across their faces as their eyes meet hers. They whoop, hurrah and wave their pom-poms.
There are three races: the qualifying race, the semifinals and the final race for Grand Champion.

Feather lines up with the other dogs for the qualifying race.
She runs as fast as she can and surprises even herself, when she is chosen as one of the qualifying winners.
Avatar was first to qualify. He beat all the dogs in the competition.
In the second race, the semifinals, Feather races against Avatar and fifty other dogs.
Avatar, once again, is far in the lead and wins first place. Feather races hard and comes in fourth place.
Only five dogs remain for the final race, including Avatar and Feather.

"The final race," Egress boasts. "Our little Feather is in the final race—the race for Grand Champion!"
"Come on Feather," cheers her family. "You can do it." Before Feather lines up, she dashes over to Lucy.
"I'm your legs today, Lucy. I'm running this race for you, my BFF."

Feather returns to post position #2. Avatar stands in post position #1.
Avatar paws the ground to mark his area of combat. Dust fills the air. The whistle blows.
Avatar explodes out of the gate and quickly takes the lead.
Feather blinks the dust from her eyes, breaks from her post and charges down the stretch.

She passes several dogs in front of her:
head held high and ears pricked forward, she passes the fourth dog in front, then the third.
Feather sprints toward Avatar on the backstretch and leaves the other dogs mere specks in the distance.

Everyone can feel the excitement and tension coming from the grandstand.
Feather's family cheers louder and louder.
The pugs scream, "Go, Feather! Go!" They bounce out of their seats and hysterically wave their pom-poms in the air.
They bark and howl with booming woof sounds. "Woof-woof, ruff-ruff, arf-arf."
"Go! Feather! Go!" Max yells. "You can do it Feather. You can do it!"

Feather passes the second place dog and propels herself alongside Avatar, who's in the lead.
Feather and Avatar turn the corner into the homestretch and charge down the track together, neck and neck.
Feather and Avatar blaze a path into racing folklore.
Lucy tries to calm the racing of her heart as she watches Feather come down the final stretch.
She lifts her foreleg and paw and lets out a high-pitched howl,
"Aaahherrrooooooooooooooooooooooo!"

Feather focuses straight ahead and never bats an eye. She takes a deep breath. "This is for you, Lucy."

Feather launches herself forward, running as fast as she can. Inch by inch, she passes Avatar.
First, half-a-head, then a full head. In the last seconds, just down to the wire,
Feather passes Avatar and crosses the finish line.

"A blanket finish, Ladies, Gentlemen and Canines!" shouts the Judge.
"Feather, only seven months old—the long-shot—has clearly upset the race today to beat Avatar,
reigning champion for the past two years." The roaring crowd goes wild.
Feather's fans swarm her for autographs as she's taken to the winner's circle.
When the Judge places the gold medal, engraved with Grand Champion, around her neck, everyone gasps.
Feather's small frame is barely visible.

Feather peeks out from behind the medal to see the people; first, from the left side, then from the right side.
Stretching tall, she peeks over the top of the medal, raises her small paw high in the air and smiles.
Deafening cheers come from the crowd as they progressively stand and do 'The Wave' across the bleachers
and shout, "Feather! Feather! Feather!" Paparazzi click and flash their cameras.

Feather sees her family rush to her, barking, jumping and cheering.
Max's hands spin the wheels of his wheelchair close behind, with Lucy tucked in his lap.
Their excitement is contagious.
"You're the winner. We're so proud of you. You are the Grand Champion!"
Avatar approaches Feather. "Great race, Feather. You're an incredibly fast and amazing little pup,
a surprise to us all." Avatar shakes her paw and strolls back into the crowd.

Lucy blinks back her tears and gives Feather a hug. "Thanks Grand Champion."
She looks at the gold medal covering Feather's chest. "Your medal is almost as big as your heart.
Thank you for running the race for me—and for all rescue animals—just like us. You are my BFF."
The Newspaper Headlines the next day read:
Local Cinderella Story
"Feather"
The pup that beat the odds
Rescue to Grand Champion

Winning Rescues

FEATHER

LUCY

Thousands of dogs just like Feather and Lucy
are abused, neglected and left without a home.
What can you do to change the life of a rescue?
Is there a Feather or Lucy waiting for you to love?

KIPPY

EGRESS